the MiLO & JAZZ MYSTERIES®

7

THE CASE OF THE PURPLE POOL

by Lewis B. Montgomery
illustrated by Amy Wummer

The KANE PRESS
New York

Text copyright © 2011 by Lewis B. Montgomery
Illustrations copyright © 2011 by Amy Wummer
Super Sleuthing Strategies original illustrations copyright © 2011 by Kane Press, Inc.
Super Sleuthing Strategies original illustrations by Nadia DiMattia

Library of Congress Cataloging-in-Publication Data

Montgomery, Lewis B.
The case of the purple pool / by Lewis B. Montgomery ; illustrated by Amy Wummer.
p. cm. — (The Milo & Jazz mysteries ; 7)
Summary: Detectives-in-training Milo and Jazz must put their skills to the test to
solve the mystery of how the water in the town swimming pool turned purple.
ISBN 978-1-57565-343-3 (library binding) — ISBN 978-1-57565-342-6 (pbk.) —
ISBN 978-1-57565-364-8 (e-book)
[1. Swimming pools—Fiction. 2. Mystery and detective stories.] I. Wummer, Amy, ill.
II. Title.
PZ7.M7682Cav 2011
[Fic]—dc22
2010051099

1 3 5 7 9 10 8 6 4 2

First published in the United States of America in 2011 by Kane Press, Inc.
Printed in the United States of America
WOZ0711

Book Design: Edward Miller

The Milo & Jazz Mysteries is a registered trademark of Kane Press, Inc.

www.kanepress.com

For Cassidy, Marina, Fiora, Zoë, Maeve,
Alexandria, Vivien, Ryujin, Cassandra, Abe,
Sierra, Annabel, Olivia, Elise, Nate, Sam,
Sophia, Julia, Evie, Meredith, Porter, Dillon,
Bridget, Leo, Sing'a, Elena, Egan, Sadie,
Cassie, Liam, and Ben. See you at the pool!
—L.B.M.

CHAPTER ONE

Milo stuffed his clothes in the locker, grabbed his beach towel, and grinned. His first day back!

Wait till the kids at the pool saw all the swimming stuff he'd learned at camp. His cannonball was totally—

"Hey, Milo!"

His friend Spencer walked into the locker room. With him was a tall blond boy Milo had never seen before.

"This is Noah," Spencer said. "He just moved here a week ago."

"Where from?" Milo asked.

Noah shook his hair back from his eyes. "California."

"Sand and sun!" Spencer spread out his arms, pretending to surf. "Catching waves! My family went on a trip to California once. It was *amazing*." He clapped Noah

on the shoulder. "Bet you can show us some great swimming tricks, huh?"

"I can do a cannonball now," Milo said.

"Cannonball! That's nothing," Spencer said. "In California, I saw a guy doing a triple somersault—off a *cliff*!"

Noah dug in Spencer's duffel bag and pulled two swimsuits out. "Hey, Spence, which one's for me?"

"The orange one is bigger." Spencer turned to Milo. "The movers lost the box with Noah's bathing suits. He hasn't been able to swim since they moved in! So I'm lending him one of mine."

"Milo! Come *on*!"

The sound of a girl's voice at the locker room door made them jump.

"That's Jazz," Milo explained.

"Your sister?" Noah asked.

"No, just a friend."

Jazz was more than just a friend, actually. She was his partner. Milo and Jazz were sleuths in training. Together, they solved real cases—with a little help from lessons they got in the mail from world-famous private eye Dash Marlowe.

Milo hurried out to meet Jazz.

She stood waiting, tapping a purple-flowered clog. "What took so long? I thought the mildew crawled off the wall and grabbed you."

Milo laughed. "No, just Spencer. And a new boy—from *California*," he added glumly, thinking of the triple somersault. So much for the tricks he'd learned at camp!

Jazz shot him a puzzled look. But all
she said was, "Let's stop by the snack bar.
I need to get my goggles from Vanessa."

At the snack bar, a teenage boy was
cooking up some corn dogs. He wore a
big, floppy, flowered sun hat and a pair
of purple swim goggles.

"Hey, Ben," Jazz greeted him. "How come you've got my goggles on?"

A voice floated up. "He's my model."

They peered over the counter. Jazz's older sister sat cross-legged on the concrete floor, surrounded by paints and crumpled paper.

"I need my goggles back," Jazz said.

Vanessa frowned. "But I'm not fin— Oh, forget it." She dropped her brush. "It's no good anyway."

"What is it?" Milo asked.

"My final project. For my summer painting class. I just can't seem to do anything with this theme."

10

"Why? What's the theme?"

"Fun in the Sun," Vanessa said unhappily.

"That doesn't sound so hard," Milo said. "Swimming, picnics, volleyball . . ."

"But that's so *obvious*," Vanessa said. "Everyone will be doing that. I want to do something *different*."

Ben turned from the fryer. "Don't worry. You'll come up with something. That last picture you painted was terrific. I totally could tell it was a cow."

Vanessa gave him a weak smile. "Ben, you're sweet."

Blushing, he turned away again. Then, looking past Milo and Jazz, his face changed.

"Oh, no. Here comes trouble."

CHAPTER TWO

A muscular young man swaggered toward the snack bar. He carried a clipboard and wore a whistle around his neck.

Jazz nudged Milo. "It's Chip!"

Milo and Jazz had met Chip on their first case, helping Jazz's older brother Dylan find his lucky socks. Chip was crazy about two things: sports and Chip. Not in that order, though.

Chip didn't seem to notice them as he leaned over the counter. When he saw

Vanessa on the floor, he frowned. "Hey! You're getting paid to work. Shouldn't you be frying fries, or popping . . . popsicles, or something?"

"It's fine," Ben said quickly. "I've got everything covered."

"This is a pool," Chip told them. "Not a—a—painting place."

"What's it to you?" Ben asked. "You're not in charge of the snack bar. You're a lifeguard."

Puffing up his chest, Chip said, "*Head* lifeguard now. That's like assistant manager of the whole pool, practically."

Vanessa pushed up to her feet. "Sorry. I shouldn't have asked Ben to model during work."

Now Chip looked interested. "Model?"

Gathering up her paints, Vanessa nodded. "For my painting."

Chip eyed the other boy's getup. Flushing, Ben snatched the floppy hat off his head. He pulled the goggles off and handed them to Jazz.

Chip turned back to Vanessa. "Looks to me like you could use a better model." He flexed his arms and flashed her a smile full of big white teeth.

Watching him, Ben scowled.

Jazz spoke up. "Chip, what's that . . . *thing* stuck in your hair?"

Chip's hands flew to his head. "What? Where?" He pulled a  little mirror from his pocket and twisted around, trying to see. Jazz pointed.

"There. No, there. No, you're still missing it. Better go look in the big mirror in the locker room."

Chip rushed away.

Puzzled, Milo said, "I didn't see anything in his hair."

Jazz smiled. "Neither did I."

Ben wasn't smiling. "Practically assistant manager," he grumbled. "I wouldn't put that guy in charge of a wading pool."

Noah came up to the counter, followed by Spencer.

"I'd like a hamburger, please," Noah said. "No, make that two."

"Two burgers?" Spencer asked. "You'll be too full to swim!"

"I'll be okay. I'm starving."

Milo introduced Noah to Jazz. Then, after finding a clear spot in the grass to spread their towels, he and Jazz walked to the pool's edge.

"On the count of three?" Jazz asked.

He nodded. "One—two—*three*."

SPLASH!

Once the first shock had passed, the water didn't feel so cold. Milo and Jazz were doing handstands when Spencer joined them.

"Where's Noah?" Milo asked.

"Over there, with Carlos." Spencer pointed.

Milo saw their school friend talking to the new boy. Two little girls in matching swimsuits tugged on Carlos's arms.

"Carlos has to babysit the twins again," Spencer said, shaking his head.

Milo groaned in sympathy. Watching his own little brother, Ethan, could be bad enough. But *twins*!

"I think they're cute," Jazz said. She was the youngest in her family. "What's wrong with them?"

"What's wrong is Carlos never gets to swim," Spencer explained. "He has to watch Mina and Fina in the baby pool."

"Don't you ever help him?" Jazz asked.

Spencer looked baffled. "Me? Why?"

Jazz rolled her eyes. "Come on, Milo. Let's go ask Carlos if he wants us to watch the twins for a while so he can swim."

"We just got in!" Milo protested. But Jazz gave him a look that made him climb out and follow her. When they reached the baby pool, though, a delighted Carlos was handing the twins over to Noah.

Jazz smiled at the new boy. "I'm glad *someone* around here thinks of other people," she said as Carlos sped away.

Noah shrugged. "I can't go in now anyway. Spence was right—two burgers are too much!"

"Well, I bet Carlos is glad you ate them," Milo said.

Noah nodded. "Yeah, he says it's torture coming to the pool when he can't swim. Poor guy! He told me sometimes he wishes they'd just close the whole place down."

CHAPTER THREE

The next day's forecast called for rain, so Milo and Jazz stayed in the pool until they looked like prunes. But in the morning Milo woke to sunshine pouring through his window. Another great day for a swim!

The pool didn't open till eleven, so he spent the morning working on his new model airplane. Finally it was time to go.

"Can I come?" Ethan begged.

Milo thought of Carlos and his sisters. Then he thought of Jazz and sighed. "Okay."

At least Ethan was old enough to swim.

They smeared on sunscreen, then swung by to pick up Jazz. Milo knocked, and a voice yelled, "Around back!"

Vanessa had an easel set up in the yard. Jazz was crouched in the grass in a swimsuit, her arms stuck straight out in front of her.

"What in the world are you doing?" Milo asked.

"Water skiing," Jazz said, looking pained.

"But you don't have any skis," Ethan pointed out.

"I know." Jazz straightened up and rubbed her back. "We don't have any water, either."

"You lost the pose again!" Vanessa complained.

Jazz shot her a murderous look.

Hastily, Milo said, "We're going to the pool. You want to come?"

"The pool!" Vanessa exclaimed, glancing at her watch. "Oh, no! I'm going to be late for work!"

"Won't Ben cover for you?" Jazz asked.

Frantically folding her easel, Vanessa shook her head. "It's his day off."

She gathered up her things and zoomed off on her bicycle. Milo waited for Jazz to get her pool bag. Then, with Ethan trailing along, they followed on foot.

When they reached the pool, they found a crowd milling around outside.

Spotting Spencer with Carlos and the twins, Milo went over. "What's going on?"

"The gate's still locked," Spencer said.

"Maybe the pool's not opening today," Carlos said cheerfully.

Mina—or was it Fina?—burst into a wail.

Milo checked his watch. It was fifteen minutes past opening time. "Is anyone inside?"

As if in answer, the gate swung open and Chip came out. The crowd surged forward.

Chip held his hands up to stop them. He announced, "The water-quality test results are inconclusive, which indicates a need to test for—uh, for more conclusive test results."

There was a puzzled silence. Then an angry-looking mom called out, "What's that supposed to mean?"

Chip shot her an uneasy glance. "It means . . . the pool is closed."

Fina—or was it Mina?—started crying. Grumbles and mutters spread through the crowd. The angry mom demanded to know where the manager was.

Mumbling something about "chain of

command," Chip fled back inside.

"There's Vanessa," Jazz said. "Maybe she knows what's wrong."

Vanessa stood at the bike rack talking to Ben. As Jazz and Milo came up, he was saying, "So, um . . . now that you don't have to work today—"

"I know, isn't it great?" Vanessa yanked her bike out and hopped on. "Now I have more time to work on my painting!"

With a wave, she pedaled off. Ben gazed after her, his mouth still hanging open.

"Ben, do you know why the pool is closed?" Jazz asked.

"Huh?" He looked at her. "Oh. No." He jerked a thumb toward the gate. "Ask Mister Practically-the-Pool-Manager, why don't you?"

Milo followed Jazz over to the tall wooden fence. They peered through the cracks between the slats.

"I can't see anything," he complained.

Jazz stepped back from the fence. "Let's walk around," she said. "Maybe there's a better place to see through."

Around the side, they found a spot where two slats had pulled slightly apart. They peeked through.

Chip stood at the edge of the pool, staring down into the water as if he had seen a shark circling.

Milo and Jazz stared at the water, too. Then, at the same time, they both burst out:

"It's *PURPLE*!"

CHAPTER FOUR

The water in the pool had always been a light, bright blue. Pool color. But now, it was definitely . . .

"Purple," Milo said again. "Wow!"

Hearing him, Chip looked up. He marched over. "No pool today, kids. Go on home." He tried to wave them away.

Jazz put her nose up to the fence. "Why is the pool that color?"

"It's technical," Chip told her. "We need to test the chlorine level and the, uh . . ." He scanned his clipboard. "Total dissolved solids . . . alkalinity . . ."

"You mean, you don't know?" Jazz said.

"Well, it was fine this morning!" Chip slumped. "My first week as head lifeguard, and this happens."

Milo couldn't help feeling sorry for him. The look on Chip's face reminded him of Ethan the time his favorite dino action-figure got stuck in the vacuum—

Ethan!

"We forgot my brother!"

Milo ran back to the gate, with Jazz close behind. To Milo's relief, Ethan was still there, along with Spencer and Carlos and his sisters. Mina and Fina had stopped crying and were begging Carlos to take them to the playground.

"Want to come?" Carlos asked Spencer. "The twins can play in the sandbox while we skateboard. I want to try out that new ramp." He zoomed his hand up through the air and grinned.

Spencer glanced toward the locked gate. He sighed. "I guess."

"Hey, guys. What's up?"

It was Noah, in a new surfer-style swim suit, a towel slung over his shoulder.

"Bad news," Spencer said gloomily. "The pool is closed today."

"You're kidding! How come?" Noah asked.

"It turned purple," Jazz said.

Six heads swiveled toward her.

"Purple?"

Milo and Jazz described what they had seen through the fence.

"I never heard of a purple pool," Carlos said.

"Me neither," Jazz told him. "And I'm the queen of purple."

That's for sure, Milo thought. Jazz
had more purple stuff than anyone he'd
ever met. Even her detective notebook
was purple. And she wrote in it with a
sparkly purple pen.

"You two should investigate!" Spencer
said.

"Investigate?" Noah asked.

"Jazz and Milo are detectives,"
Spencer explained to the new boy.
"They solved a mystery about my parrot,
Floyd." He turned to them. "I'll bet you
could solve this one, too!"

Milo and Jazz looked at each other.

"I don't know if it's a *mystery*," Milo
said. "Something probably just went
wrong with the pool chemicals."

Slowly, Jazz nodded. "Yeah . . . Chip

will call the manager, and they'll figure it out. Right?"

Ethan wanted to go to the playground too, so they all went off together. Jazz split off from the group, saying she had stuff to do.

When Milo got home, he found a message to call Jazz. She answered on the first ring.

"Guess what?" Jazz announced. "Pools don't turn purple."

"Huh? But we saw—"

"I mean, they don't turn purple *accidentally*. I looked it up. They can turn green or yellow, if there isn't enough chlorine in the water. But not purple."

"Then how did it get that color?" Milo asked.

"I'm not sure," Jazz admitted. "But I think it was some kind of dye."

"A dye? But that means . . ."

"Someone turned the pool purple on purpose! And *that* means . . ."

Milo grinned. He knew exactly what his partner was about to say.

"We've got a case!"

CHAPTER FIVE

The pool reopened the next day. A sign at the front desk said the purple water was safe to swim in. The color was filtering out, and soon it would be back to normal.

Jazz dipped a toe in the pool. "It's not really purple anymore. More like . . . lavender. Or lilac."

"I don't care if it's polka dot," Milo grumbled. He was stinging from the brush-off they had gotten when they tried to question the pool manager. He bet nobody ever told Dash Marlowe, "Run along!"

"Here comes Chip," Jazz said. "Let's talk to him."

Chip still carried his clipboard, but he'd lost some of his swagger. He eyed them glumly.

"What's wrong?" Jazz asked.

"The manager chewed me out," Chip said. "She said if I paid as much attention to the pool as I did to my hair, it would still be blue."

"Your hair?" Milo asked.

"The *pool*." Chip looked injured. "I don't see how it's my fault."

Jazz said, "What happened, exactly? You came in to open up the pool . . ."

Chip nodded. "Right on time. The water looked perfectly normal. I went through the list—"

"The list?" Jazz asked.

"My checklist of jobs to do." He tapped his clipboard.

Peering over his elbow, Jazz skimmed through the list. "Locker rooms," she read aloud.

39

"That's when it happened," Chip said. "I went in to tidy up. When I came out, the pool was purple!"

"How long were you in there?" Milo asked.

"Ten minutes. Fifteen, tops. Well . . . I don't know."

Milo glanced sideways at Jazz, thinking of the mirrors in the locker rooms. Chip loved looking at himself.

Jazz said, "So anyone could have walked in—"

"But they couldn't!" Chip said. "I locked the gate behind me. It has to stay locked until opening time."

"Does anyone else have a key?" Jazz asked.

"The manager. That's all."

A big splash and shrieking interrupted them. "No horseplay!" Chip yelled, striding off.

Puzzled, Milo looked at Jazz. "You don't think the manager . . ."

Jazz shook her head. "I doubt it. And I don't think Chip did it either. He seems too upset."

"But nobody else has a key." Milo pointed to the fence. "And look how high that fence is. Nothing to hold onto, either. It would be tough to climb over that."

"Maybe Chip forgot to lock the gate behind him?" Jazz said.

"Maybe," he agreed.

She frowned. "But who would want to turn the pool purple?"

"Someone who likes purple?" He

narrowed his eyes. "Where were *you* yesterday morning?"

"Milo! Be serious!"

He grinned. "Seriously . . . I'm hungry. Let's go get a snack."

"Already?" Jazz rolled her eyes.

As they walked across the concrete, Milo added, "Anyway, whoever put the purple in won't do it again."

"Why not?" Jazz asked.

"Because it got the pool closed for a whole day!" he said. "Nobody wants that."

Jazz stopped short. "That's it!"

"What?"

"Maybe someone *wanted* to shut down the pool," she said.

He frowned. "How come?"

"I don't know. But if they did, turning it purple worked."

Hmm. She had a point.

Chip had gotten to the snack bar ahead of them. He leaned against the counter, smiling at Vanessa as Ben glowered in the background.

As they came up, Milo heard Chip say, "I think this is my better side, don't you?" He struck a profile.

"Cheered up fast, didn't he?" Milo said to Jazz.

She didn't answer.

"Jazz?" He turned.

A few steps behind him, she stood frozen and staring—straight at Ben.

CHAPTER SIX

"Are you okay?" Milo asked.

Jazz didn't answer. Instead, she marched up to the counter. "Ben, wasn't yesterday your day off?"

Tearing his eyes away from Vanessa and Chip, Ben turned. "Huh? Um . . . yeah."

"Then how come you were here?"

Ben looked startled. "What?"

"You were here," Jazz pressed. "When we found out that the pool was closed. But it was your day off. Vanessa said so."

Ben shot a glance at Vanessa. Chip had moved on to talk to the lifeguard on duty, and Vanessa was busy grilling burgers. As Ben looked at her, a red flush crept up his neck.

"I just stopped by for a minute," he mumbled. "I had stuff to take care of."

"What kind of stuff?"

Ben turned even redder. "Stuff. Just stuff. Okay?"

Before Jazz could push further, Milo dragged her away.

"Why did you do that?" she said. "I was really getting somewhere."

"Yeah. Getting on his nerves," Milo said. "It looked to me like you might get a corn dog up the nose."

"Don't you think it's suspicious? Ben wasn't supposed to be here, but he came in anyway—right around the time the pool turned purple."

"But why would he want to close the pool down on his day off?"

Jazz frowned, then brightened. "Maybe to get Vanessa off work, too. I think Ben wants to ask my sister out."

Milo thought that was the dumbest reason he had ever heard. Still, it was possible. Teenagers did weird things.

"Ben doesn't like Chip much," Milo pointed out. "Maybe he did it to get Chip in trouble."

Jazz nodded. "Or maybe both. How can we prove it, though?"

Milo pictured her trying to wring a confession out of an angry Ben. Quickly, he said, "We don't know for sure that it was Ben. We should look for clues."

"Like what?"

He thought. "Well, how did he get in without a key? Maybe if we peek in his backpack, we'll find lock-picking tools."

"Maybe." She looked doubtful. "Or he could have sneaked the key away from

Chip. Or maybe there's a place where you can crawl under the fence?"

"Fine. Show me, then," Milo said grumpily. He still felt hungry. Why couldn't Jazz have let him get a bag of chips before she started bugging Ben?

Not wanting the lifeguards to notice them, they left the pool area and circled the fence from the outside. Jazz walked slowly, looking closely at the bottom of the fence.

Milo slapped a mosquito away. He felt hot and sticky. Peeking through the fence, he spotted Spencer, ready to jump off the high dive. The water below looked cool and inviting, though still faintly purple.

"Milo! Look at this!" Jazz crouched near the fence, pointing at something in

the grass. Milo went over to look.

"Purple dribbles!" he said.

Jazz nodded. "This must be where
Ben—or somebody—got in." She eyed
the fence. "But how? There's nowhere to
squeeze under here."

"Maybe he didn't actually get in. He could have thrown the dye over the top."

"How? In a bottle?"

"Sure," Milo said. "Or a balloon. Like a water bomb."

"But wouldn't they have found it in the pool?" Jazz asked.

Milo thought of his airplane kit. "What if he *flew* it over in one of those little airplanes? By remote control? And did a loop-de-loop to dump it out—"

"Oh, Milo." Sighing, Jazz flopped backward in the grass, staring up at the branches of the tree above her.

An instant later, she sprang to her feet again. Before Milo could ask what she was doing, she was scrambling up the tree.

"Uh . . . Jazz?"

"Hang on!" she called down. "I'm looking . . ."

He craned his neck. "Looking for what?"

No answer. Then, just as he was about to ask again, her voice floated down.

"Wow. I can't believe it. Wow. Milo! Come up and see!"

CHAPTER SEVEN

Milo clambered up the tree. He could see Jazz through the branches above him, dangling something big and floppy.

Hauling himself up next to her, he saw what it was: a long, skinny plastic tube wound up like a garden hose. It had been clear, but now it was stained purple.

"You were right," Jazz said. "Ben didn't need to get in the pool area at all. He climbed the tree, poked the tube over the fence, and poured the purple dye straight down the tube into the pool. He pulled the tube back out—"

"Dribbling purple on the grass," Milo put in.

"—then rolled it up, left it in the tree, and walked away," Jazz finished. "Pretty smart, huh?"

"Yeah, but we caught him!" Milo said. "I can't wait to show the manager." He reached for the tube.

Jazz pulled it away. "No. It stays here."

"But it's evidence—"

"It proves *how* the pool got turned purple," Jazz said. "It doesn't tell us *who*."

"Fingerprints?" Milo said.

"Anyone that clever probably wore gloves." She shook her head. "Besides, I've got a better idea."

"What?"

Instead of answering, Jazz asked, "Why would Ben leave the tube behind?"

Milo shrugged. "He's a litterbug?"

His partner smiled. "Or maybe he was planning to come back and *turn the pool purple again.*"

"You mean—"

Jazz nodded. "We need to stake out the tree and catch him in the act."

"But how do we know when he's going to come back?" Milo asked. "I don't think our parents would be happy if we started living in a tree."

Milo & Jazz
Large Maple Tree
Westview Town Pool

She frowned. "Well . . . yesterday it happened in the morning. . . ."

Milo leaned against the tree trunk, thinking. "Maybe we could smoke Ben out. You know, do something to make him come back."

"Like what?"

Milo grinned. "Watch me."

Leaving the plastic tube behind, they

climbed down the tree. Milo led the way to the snack bar, where Vanessa and Ben were dealing with a late-afternoon rush.

Spencer and Noah stood in line ahead of them. Spencer was saying, "Swimmer's ear? I had that once. Itched like crazy!"

"Mine isn't so bad," Noah said. "I just can't go in the deep end for a while." The girl in front of them left with an ice-cream bar, and Noah stepped up to order from Ben.

Milo nudged Jazz. "Here goes." He raised his voice. "Those police really work fast, don't they?"

Jazz looked at him. "Uh . . . yeah!"

"I mean, the pool only turned purple yesterday, and they already have a suspect," he went on loudly. "Chip says

57

they've almost nailed it. They just have
to find one thing."

"Really?" Jazz said. "What?"

"Chip didn't say." He sneaked a glance
at Ben, then bellowed, "SOMETHING
TO DO WITH HOW THE PURPLE
STUFF GOT IN THE POOL."

Milo turned to peek at Ben again. Ben
was staring straight at him.

Just then, a voice behind Milo said,
"You don't have to shout." He spun
around.

It was Carlos. Milo stared.

Over his trunks, Carlos wore a white
T-shirt. At least, it had once been white.
Now it had stains all down the front.

Big, splotchy, *purple* stains.

CHAPTER EIGHT

"What?" Following Milo's gaze, Carlos glanced down at his stained shirt. "Oh, yeah . . ." He smiled in an embarrassed way. "Fina shot me with her grape juice. I keep telling those girls not to hold their juice boxes so tight."

Speechless, Milo nodded.

"What's with all the yelling?" Carlos asked. He looked at Jazz. "You two having a fight?"

"No," Jazz said, "We were just—"

"We have to go!" Milo cut in.

He dragged Jazz out of earshot to the far end of the pool.

"What was that about?" she said.

"Didn't you see his shirt?"

"He said it was grape juice."

"That doesn't mean it's true," Milo argued. "And Carlos *wanted* to shut down the pool. Remember? Noah said he hated having to bring the twins here and not getting to swim. He said that he'd be happier if they just closed it down."

Jazz glanced back toward Carlos. "He was probably exaggerating."

Milo shook his head. "Didn't you notice? When Chip said the pool was closed, Carlos was the only one who didn't seem upset. He seemed pretty happy to go skateboarding."

Jazz looked thoughtful. "That's true."

"So now we have two suspects," Milo said. "What do we do?"

"Nothing," Jazz said.

"Nothing?"

"I mean, nothing different," she told him. "Both of them heard you, right?"

"I guess so."

"You *guess* so? I bet people heard you two towns over," Jazz said. "So, we do what we were going to do anyway. Stake out the tree. And see who comes."

They decided the culprit probably wouldn't go back for the tube while the pool was open. He'd wait till everyone was gone to get rid of the evidence.

It was almost dinnertime, so Milo and Jazz split up. They agreed to meet back at the tree just before the pool closed.

When Milo got home, he found an envelope addressed to him with *DM* in the corner. A new sleuthing lesson from Dash Marlowe!

DASH MARLOWE

SECRETS OF A SUPER SLEUTH!

Infer

Hidden corners. Dark, deserted alleys. Midnight break-ins.

Criminals are sneaky. They don't like to do their dirty deeds out in the open, where they can be seen. And so, as sleuths, we often have to depend on **circumstantial evidence**.

Circumstantial evidence is not direct. It's not absolute proof. But it can help us infer what happened. (To **infer** means to look at the evidence you have, think carefully about it, and then draw a conclusion.)

Suppose you saw a man shoot another man. That would be direct evidence. You know what happened, because you saw it with your own eyes.

But suppose you hear a shot. You arrive on the scene a few moments later. . . . You see a man lying on the ground. Another man stands over him, holding a smoking gun. That's circumstantial evidence.

You can build a strong case around circumstantial evidence. However, you need to be careful, too. What you infer may be what actually took place—or it may not.

Take the example of the smoking gun. What if there were three men? The first man shot the second. Then he tossed the gun to the third man and ran away.

Or maybe there were just two men—and a grizzly bear. One man shot off his gun, scaring the grizzly away. The other man, terrified by the gunshot and the bear, had a heart attack and collapsed.

Speaking of bears and shooting, I'll never forget The Case of the Gunslinging Grizzly—

But that's another story.

At dinner, Milo hardly tasted his homemade pizza. He kept thinking about Dash's lesson.

Ben and Carlos both had motives to close down the pool. And they had both been at the pool the morning it turned purple.

Ben being there on his day off was suspicious. Carlos being there was normal. After all, lots of kids had come to swim that day. Still—he was there.

All the evidence Milo and Jazz had was circumstantial. If their stakeout was successful, though, they'd nab Carlos or Ben trying to make off with the evidence.

And once he'd been caught in the act, Milo was sure, the culprit would confess.

CHAPTER NINE

Jazz was already up in the tree when Milo got there. Checking first to make sure nobody was watching, he climbed up too.

The pool was nearly empty now. Parents were folding beach towels and dragging shrieking little kids off to the locker rooms.

Vanessa stood talking to Chip, who was acting odd. First he stood with one hand down and one up to his shoulder. Then he raised one arm and gazed into the distance.

"What in the world is he doing?" Milo asked.

Jazz giggled. "Posing! I think he wants Vanessa to paint him."

They watched Vanessa wave goodbye to Chip. After a quick chat with Ben at the snack bar, she took off.

Handing Milo the rolled-up tube, Jazz climbed to a higher branch and peered out at the pool.

"Ben should be out any minute," Milo said. "He's almost done with—"

"*Shhh!*"

Startled, Milo looked up at Jazz. She pointed. Instead of getting on her bike and pedaling away, Vanessa was walking straight in their direction. Had she seen them?

Stopping under the tree, Vanessa glanced around.

Then it hit Milo like a flash.

Vanessa had been happy when the pool was closed yesterday. She said it gave her more time to paint.

And she'd been working at the snack bar when Milo mentioned the police. What he had said for Ben's ears, Vanessa must have heard too.

Milo glanced up at Jazz again. What would she do if the culprit turned out to be her own sister?

Jazz put a finger to her lips. Again, she pointed.

Ben was coming toward the tree.

Milo's thoughts churned in confusion. Was it Ben after all? Or Vanessa? Could the two of them be in cahoots?

"Hey, Ben," Vanessa said. "I don't see anything out here to paint."

"Paint?" Ben looked blank.

"Didn't you ask me to meet you here so we could talk about Fun in the Sun?"

"Oh—yeah, I did. But not the way you mean . . . I wanted to talk to you alone, away from Chip, so I . . ." Ben paused, then tried again. "Vanessa, I was wondering if you would like to—"

He broke off.

Someone had come around the corner of the fence. A boy. He saw the teenagers and stopped, looking uncertain.

It was Noah.

Milo leaned out a little further. Now, what was *he*—

"AAAAAAAAAHH!" Milo yelled as the branch under his hand snapped. As he grabbed another branch, he dropped the tube.

Noah stared at the tube on the ground. He shot a panicked glance up at the tree. Then he turned and fled.

Ignoring Ben's and Vanessa's startled shouts, Milo scrambled down the tree.

"Stop!" he yelled.

Noah sped up. Milo chased after him as Jazz pounded behind.

The parking lot was full of people—kids unlocking their bikes, families climbing into cars. Noah ran across the walk. At that moment, Vanessa and Ben came around the fence from the other direction.

Trapped on three sides, Noah looked around wildly. Then he turned and ran through the gate into the pool area, with Milo close behind.

Chip stood by the pool, skimming
stray leaves off the surface.

"Stop him!" Milo yelled.

Noah, still running, shot a
panicked glance over his shoulder.

Startled, Chip spun around.

Milo saw it all in slow
motion: Chip, body
twisted, one foot
raised. Noah,
head turned
away, plowing
into him. And
Chip, arms
flailing, falling
backward into
the pool with a
gigantic splash.

Noah sprawled on the pool deck. Milo jumped on top of him, pinning him down. He didn't struggle.

"You have the right to remain silent," Milo gasped. "But you'd better talk, or else!"

Noah groaned. "Okay," he admitted. "I did it. I put the purple pool dye in the water."

Milo let him up. Jazz, Ben, and Vanessa clustered around.

"But why?" Jazz asked.

Noah hung his head. "It was . . . well . . . because of Spence, I guess."

"*Spencer* made you do it?" Milo said, shocked.

"He didn't know anything about it," Noah answered quickly. "It was just . . .

Spence was so sure that anyone from California must be amazing in the water."

"You mean you can't dive off high cliffs and stuff?" Milo asked Noah.

"I can't even jump off the low board," Noah admitted miserably. "I . . . I can't swim."

"At *all?*"

Noah shook his head. Then he blurted, "I wanted to tell Spence the truth! I really did. But I was too embarrassed, so I made up an excuse about losing my swimsuit in the move. And then—well, then the next time it was even harder. I'd already told a fib. And Spence kept telling everyone what a great swimmer I was. . . ." He trailed off.

Milo thought of the time that Spencer

had decided his parrot
wanted him to be
a pirate. Spencer
was a good guy, but
sometimes he could
really get carried away.

Jazz looked at Noah.
"So then you felt kind
of stuck, didn't you? You had to keep
making more excuses not to go in the
pool. Eating too much, watching the
twins—"

"Swimmer's ear," Milo said,
remembering.

Noah nodded. "That was a good one.
Too bad I didn't think of it before I
turned the pool purple."

"But what even gave you the idea of

dyeing it?" Jazz asked.

"I saw an ad," Noah said. "Rainbow Pool, they called it—one bottle to color a whole pool. The ad said the dye was harmless, but I figured they'd at least have to close the pool while they checked.

Now I feel like I was crazy to do it." His shoulders drooped. "I wish I'd just told the truth before making so much trouble for everyone."

"You and me both."

They all turned. Chip stood on the deck, dripping wet, a puddle forming around his feet. Wide-eyed, Noah watched as Chip squished slowly over.

He looked down at Noah.

"Kid," he said, "we need to have a talk."

CHAPTER TEN

Saturday morning was sunny and hot. Milo stood in front of a painting of a surfer. At least, he *thought* it was a surfer. It might have been someone standing up in a canoe.

"You know," Jazz said, "I've never worn a swimsuit to an art show."

"I've never worn anything to an art show," he told her. No, wait, that sounded wrong. "I mean, I've never *been* to an art show before."

Near them, Ben said to Vanessa, "That

was a great idea, getting your art teacher to hang the pictures at the pool!"

"Well, you know . . . Fun in the Sun," Vanessa said. She smiled at Ben. "Thanks for coming as my date. I was a little nervous about asking you."

Ben looked surprised. "You were? But . . ." He stopped, blushing.

"What?" Vanessa asked.

He shook his head. "Oh, just remind me to tell you something sometime." Hand in hand, they walked off together.

Ethan tugged on Milo's arm. "I like Vanessa's picture the best. It's funny!"

Milo had to agree. Sailing, surfing, and sand castles were okay. But Vanessa's painting was his favorite. She'd perfectly captured the look on Chip's face as he fell into the pool.

"I wonder how Chip likes it," Jazz whispered.

Milo shrugged. "He wanted to be a model, right? Besides, Chip likes anything that has to do with Chip."

"Hey, don't make fun of Chip!" a voice said.

They turned. It was Noah.

"I owe that guy," Noah went on. "I still

can't believe he didn't turn me in. If the manager knew what I did, she'd ban me from the pool forever."

"You mean, you *want* to go in the pool now?" Jazz asked.

Noah nodded. "Chip got me to sign up for swim class."

"He's a Polliwog, like me!" Ethan said.

Noah winced. "Just for now. By the end of the summer, I'm going to be a Shark. Or at least a Porpoise."

Milo looked at the water. It was its usual blue again. "So," he said, "The Case of the Purple Pool is closed."

Jazz turned to Noah. "We don't have to tell anyone it was you," she said. "I mean, just Dash Marlowe, when we write to him. But not Spencer or anybody else."

"I told Spence everything," Noah said.

"You did?"

"Yeah. And I explained that just because you live in California doesn't mean you go to the beach all the time. I've never even seen the beach. I'm from the mountains."

"What did he say?" Jazz asked.

"Well . . ."

"Mountain man!" Spencer said, coming up and clapping a hand on Noah's shoulder. He turned to Milo and Jazz. "Wait till winter. Noah's going to show us some serious snowboard tricks."

They looked at Noah.

"I *do* know how to snowboard," Noah said. "I'm not an expert, but—"

"Come on, I'll bet you're great!"

Spencer threw an arm around his shoulder.
As he steered Noah away, Milo heard him
say, "One time I saw a movie where a
guy jumped from a helicopter, landed on
his snowboard, and then—*whoosh*! Right
down the mountain. Did you ever . . . ?"

Milo and Jazz looked at each other. They laughed.

"Wait till Dash hears about this case," Milo said. "You think he's ever had one where a swimming pool turned purple?"

"Probably not," Jazz said. "Although I wouldn't be surprised if he had one with a guy jumping from a helicopter. The Case of the Purloined Parachute."

Milo said, "Or the Flattened Felon."

Jazz made a face. "Yuck!"

"The Squished Suspect?"

"*Milo!*"

He grinned. In a deep Dash Marlowe voice, he concluded, "But that's another story."

SUPER SLEUTHING STRATEGIES

A few days after Milo and Jazz wrote to Dash Marlowe, a letter arrived in the mail. . . .

Greetings, Milo and Jazz,

Your seventh case solved—I'm glad to see you weren't in over your heads! Hope that Noah learned you should never act as if you know how to do something when you don't. I figured that out when I pretended to be a veteran animal tamer in The Case of the Touchy Tiger. . . .

Happy Sleuthing!
—Dash Marlowe

Warm Up!
To solve those tough cases, detectives need to keep their brains in top condition. Tackle these brain stretchers and stay strong! The answers? Right at the end of this letter.

1. What can you catch but not throw?
2. What belongs to you but is mostly used by others?
3. A silly one: What do you say when you meet a two-headed monster?
4. You've been sentenced to die by the king. But you can choose the way you'll die. So what will it be? (Hint: The king didn't ask you how you wanted to be *killed*.)

The Perilous Pool: An Observation Puzzle

A purple pool is definitely a problem. But once I came across a pool with even *more* problems! I had dropped by the home of an eccentric client. While I was there, he happened to mention that fewer and fewer of his guests were using his pool. As soon as I checked it out, I could see why! Using your observation skills, take a look and see how many different problems you can pick out. . . .

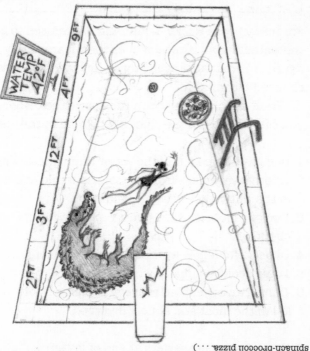

Answer: 1. Part of the rail into the pool was missing. 2. The water was awfully cold—42° F! 3. The depth numbers along the side of pool were out of order. 4. The diving board was at the shallow end of the pool. 5. The board was cracked, too. 6. A spinach-broccoli pizza was floating by. 7. A crocodile was paddling around as if he owned the place. (When I suggested that the owner get rid of the crocodile, he said, "Alfred?! No way—he's the best pet I ever had. And don't worry. He is a strict vegetarian." So that explained the spinach-broccoli pizza. . . .)

91

Don't Go Near the Water!: A Logic Puzzle

For many years Rocky, Louie, and Sal refused to go in the water, but all three got over their fears. Can you figure out what kept each guy on dry land and what changed his mind?

Read the clues and fill in the answer box where you can. Then read the clues again to fill in the rest.

1. One guy stayed out of the water after he saw *Jaws*.
2. Another guy was afraid his toupee would come off in the water and show his bald spot.
3. Rocky's mom got him shark repellant for his birthday.
4. One fearful fellow won 12 free swim lessons.
5. Louis decided it was cool to be bald.
6. During an attempted robbery of Castle Doom, Sal fell in the moat and almost drowned.

Answer box (see answers at end of letter)

	Rocky	Louie	Sal
Why he stayed dry			
What changed him			

Possibilities: An Inference Puzzle

Every detective makes lots of inferences—logical guesses. Check out these cases, and pick the inferences that sound like good possibilities. (You may choose more than one.) Then I'll reveal what the real facts were!

1. I was investigating the theft of a stunning emerald ring when I spotted it on the hand of the well-known actress Trixie Astor. What did I infer?

   a. Maybe she stole it.

   b. She got it from the thief.

   c. Green is her favorite color.

   d. It could be a copy.

2. A painting of George Washington had been slashed. What did I infer?

   a. Whoever did it hated George Washington.

   b. Whoever did it was testing a new knife.

   c. Whoever did it hated the artist.

   d. Whoever did it hated the owner.

3. I was questioning a forgery suspect who seemed very nervous—moving in his chair, unable to meet my eyes. What did I infer?

   a. He's afraid I think he's guilty

   b. He is guilty.

   c. He's just a nervous guy.

   d. A combination of all three.

Answers: 1. a, b, and d were all reasonable possibilities, but b was closest to the facts. What really happened was that the thief was the actress's chauffeur. He'd accidentally dropped the ring in the limo. She owned so much jewelry, she assumed it was hers and put it on. 2. a, c, and d were all good inferences—and they were all true! The culprit was one angry guy. 3. This case was a great reminder to me that inferences are not facts! All the inferences in this situation were logical possibilities. But it turned out that the suspect just had to go to the bathroom!

93

We Don't Byte: A Mini-Mystery

Check out this mystery—and draw a conclusion!

Valuable equipment had been stolen from a computer store, and I was called in to investigate. The main suspect was a teenage girl, but the evidence against her was all circumstantial. She was always in the store trying out the computers. A sales clerk said he'd seen the girl lurking in the alley, where a window had been broken the night of the robbery. And the girl had fresh cuts on her arm, cuts that could have come from climbing through a shattered window—though she insisted she'd hurt herself doing yard work.

I checked out the store, but found no clues other than the broken window. Then I went to the alley, where I noticed broken glass littering the ground. I had my answer. "Aha," I said. "The girl is innocent!" How did I draw that conclusion?

Answer: If the robber had broken the window to get into the store, the glass would have been *inside*, not outside. I figured the sales clerk was the real robber and had smashed the window to make it look as if an outsider had broken in. I was right!

Answer to Logic Puzzle: The movie *Jaws* made Rocky afraid of the water—until his mom bought him shark repellant. Falling into the castle moat scared Sal, but he got brave after he graduated from Polliwog to Guppy in his free swim class. Louis always felt embarrassed when his toupee came off in the water, but one day he decided to be bald and proud.

Answers for Brain Stretchers:
1. A cold
2. Your name
3. "Hello. Hello."
4. To die of old age

Praise for . . .

"**The Milo & Jazz Mysteries** is a series that parents can enjoy reading with their children, together finding the clues and deducing 'whodunit'. The end of book puzzles are a real treat and will likely challenge most readers, regardless of age level."
—*Mysterious Reviews, Hidden Staircase Mysteries*

"Certain to be a popular series, **The Milo & Jazz Mysteries** are highly recommended additions to school and community library collections for young readers." —*Midwest Book Review*

★**Book 1: The Case of the Stinky Socks**
"Gets it just right." —*Booklist*, starred review
Book Links' Best New Books for the Classroom

Book 2: The Case of the Poisoned Pig
Agatha Award Nominee for best children's mystery
"Highly recommended." —*Midwest Book Review*

Book 3: The Case of the *Haunted* Haunted House
"Builds up to an exciting finish." —*Mysterious Reviews*

Book 4: The Case of the Amazing Zelda
"Fun page-turner." —*Library Media Connection*

Book 5: The Case of the July 4th Jinx
"Quick paced, humorous, kid friendly . . . excellent summer reading for kids."
—*Midwest Book Review*

Book 6: The Case of the Missing Moose

Collect these mysteries and more—coming soon!

Visit www.kanepress.com to see all titles in The Milo & Jazz Mysteries.

ABOUT THE AUTHOR

Lewis B. Montgomery is the pen name of a writer whose favorite authors include CSL, EBW, and LMM. Those initials are a clue—but there's another clue, too. Can you figure out their names?

Besides writing the Milo & Jazz mysteries, LBM enjoys eating spicy Thai noodles and blueberry ice cream, riding a bike, and reading. Not all at the same time, of course. At least, not anymore. But that's another story. . . .

ABOUT THE ILLUSTRATOR

Amy Wummer has illustrated more than 50 children's books. She uses pencils, watercolors, and ink—but not the invisible kind.

Amy and her husband, who is also an artist, live in Pennsylvania . . . in a mysterious old house which has a secret hidden room in the basement!